For Henry, who likes brown bears
- S.S.

For Emma, a truly loyal and courageous friend who challenges her greatest
fears every day with a punch, a kick, and a giggle
- C.P.

tiger tales
5 River Road, Suite 128, Wilton, CT 06897
Published in the United States 2018
Originally published in Great Britain 2018
by Little Tiger Press
Text copyright © 2018 Steve Smallman
Illustrations copyright © 2018 Caroline Pedler
ISBN-13: 978-1-68010-100-3
ISBN-10: 1-68010-100-5
Printed in China
LTP/1400/2207/0318

For more insight and activities, visit us at www.tigertalesbooks.com

Scaredy
BEAR

by
Steve Smallman

Illustrated by
Caroline Pedler

tiger tales

Little Bob was the bravest of bunnies.
He LOVED exploring, but he DIDN'T LIKE going to bed.
"Why can't I go out and play?" he pleaded.

"Because," said his mom,
"In the deep, dark forest there's nothing as scary
As the terrible creature they call the BIG HAIRY!
He has huge, scary teeth and long, scary claws,
And it sounds just like thunder when he stomps his big paws!"

"Oooooooooooh!"
gasped Little Bob, jumping into bed,
where he stayed until . . .

. . . his mom was asleep!
Then he crept out of bed, grabbed
an extra-pointy carrot, and set
out to find the BIG HAIRY!
The forest felt strange and
spooky in the moonlight.

"Maybe I should look for
the Big Hairy another day,"
Little Bob whispered to himself.

Then he saw a shadow
that looked exactly like . . .

. . . AN OWL!

Quick as a flash, Little Bob
ran this way and that.

He dodged
and swerved,

and climbed
and **leaped**,

and just in time,
he dove under a great big bush!
But it wasn't a bush.

It was a bear.

"EEEEK!" squeaked the bear. "You scared me!"
"I'm sorry!" said Little Bob. "I'm hunting for the Big Hairy!
In all of the forest there's nothing as scary
As the terrible creature they call the BIG HAIRY!"

"He sounds awful!" gasped the bear,
who didn't want to be alone if
there was a monster around.
"Can I come with you?"

"Okay," nodded the bunny. "My name's Little Bob. What's yours?"

"I don't know," said the bear.

"What do your friends call you?" asked Little Bob.

"I don't have any friends," said the bear.

"Oh!" said Little Bob. "Well, I'll be your friend if you want, and I will call you . . . Big Bob!"

Big Bob was very excited to have a friend. "What do friends do?" he asked. "Oh, this and that . . . ," Little Bob said with a shrug.

So that's what they did until Big Bob's tummy started to rumble.

"Little Bob," he said, "do friends share their carrots?"
"Yes," said Little Bob, "but not *this* carrot. I'm going to stick *this* carrot right up the **Big Hairy's nose!**"

"Gosh!" gulped Big Bob.
"How can you be so brave when you are so small?"
"Because," Little Bob whispered,
"I'm **big** on the inside."

"I must be tiny on the inside," sighed Big Bob.
"I'm sure there's a big bear in there somewhere,"
said Little Bob, looking in Big Bob's ear.
"You just need to let him out!"

Then Little Bob's tummy rumbled, too.
"I'll get us some food," smiled Big Bob, ambling off.

It wasn't long before Little
Bob heard a noise behind him.
"That was quick!" he chuckled.
But it wasn't his friend.

It was a fox!

The fox **leaped** toward Little Bob,
and was about to gobble him up when . . .

RoARRR!

Out of the bushes came an *enormous hairy creature*.

It had *huge, scary teeth* and *long, scary claws*,

And it made the ground shake when it stomped its *big paws!*

The fox was so scared that he raced off
into the trees.

"IT'S the BIG HAIRY!"
squealed Little Bob, shaking as he
held up his extra-pointy carrot.

Then the Big Hairy stopped roaring, gave a worried smile,
and said, "Are you all right, Little Bob?"

"Big Bob! It's you!"
cried Little Bob in surprise. "You're the Big Hairy!"

"I can't be," said Big Bob. "I'm just a scaredy bear."
"It's the big bear inside you," beamed Little Bob.
"You let it out!"

"Oh, no!" gasped Big Bob.
"Does that mean . . ."

"... you're going to stick your carrot up my nose?"

Little Bob looked up at his friend's worried face
and started to giggle. Then he started to laugh.
Soon Big Bob was laughing, too.

And, when they were all
laughed out, they shared the
extra-pointy carrot for dinner.

"What should we do now, Big Bob?" yawned Little Bob.
"I think it's time for you to go home," said Big Bob.
"But can we still be friends tomorrow?"
"Of course!" said Little Bob. "We can be friends forever!"
Big Bob smiled and the two friends wandered off, chatting
about this and that, all the way home to bed.